# SPOOKY AND THE GHOST CAT

by Natalie Savage Carlson    illustrated by Andrew Glass

Lothrop, Lee & Shepard Books

New York

*For Michelle and Laura Bushey,*
*the miracle twins*

Library of Congress Cataloging in Publication Data/Carlson, Natalie Savage. Spooky and the ghost cat. Summary: On Halloween night, Spooky, a black cat, rescues a ghost cat from a witch to whom he once belonged.
1. Children's stories, American. [1. Cats—Fiction. 2. Witches—Fiction.  3. Halloween—Fiction]  I. Glass, Andrew, ill.
II. Title.  PZ7.C2167Sou  1985      [E]      84-17146      ISBN 0-688-04316-X      ISBN 0-688-04317-8 (lib. bdg.)
Typography by Lynn Braswell

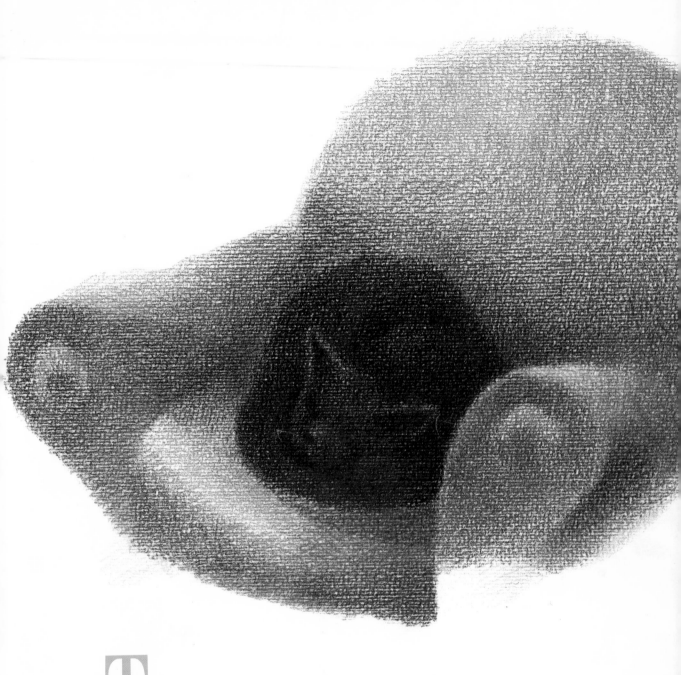

The Bascombs had a big black cat named Spooky. He had once belonged to a witch. But now he was a real pet. Spooky liked to lie in the fat chair with the bump in the seat and *purrr, purprpr, pur-r-r.*

One night the Bascomb girl came home from a movie.

She said to her family, "There was a white cat on the porch, but when I leaned over to pet her, nothing was there."

"Perhaps she was a ghost," joked the Bascomb father.

"She must belong to a witch," joked the Bascomb boy.

That night when the Bascombs were asleep, Spooky jumped down from the chair. He went pussyfoot, pussyfoot into the kitchen.

He pushed through the little hinged door that had been cut into the big door.

It was a cool fall night. Dead leaves fluttered down. There was a smell of wood smoke in the air. A wishbone of wild geese crossed the moon.

Spooky went pussyfoot, pussyfoot through the yard and jumped up on the fence. He was surprised to see a pretty white cat sitting not far from him.

Spooky liked her looks. His whiskers twitched and his tail switched. He began to show off for her.

Spooky stood up on his hind paws and stretched toward the moon. He stood up on his front paws and pointed his tail at the moon. The ghost cat seemed happy.

But when Spooky moved over to tickle her nose with his whiskers, she slowly faded away. Spooky looked here

and there

and elsewhere for her.

Suddenly she appeared again.

They romped together. They rolled in the crackly leaves. They chased one another. But when Spooky caught the white cat, *nothing* was in his paws.

Then the mysterious cat left the yard. She went down the road tippy-toe, tippy-toe. Spooky followed her pussyfoot, pussyfoot.

They came to the woods at the end of the road. The white cat went into them tippy-toe. Spooky stopped. The witch to whom Spooky had once belonged lived in the woods. Had she sent the ghost cat to bring him back?

"*Pfft, pfft!*" He spat at the witch, although she wasn't there. He knew the witch was keeping the white cat under a spell, but he didn't dare to go into the woods.

He went home with his tail dragging. He howled and yowled and squalled in disappointment. A window flew open and an old brush was thrown at him.

The next night was Halloween. A jack-o-lantern moon hung high. The trick or treaters had gone home with bags of goodies and all was as still as a graveyard.

Spooky went pussyfoot, pussyfoot down the road to look for the ghost cat. He soon reached the edge of the woods. An owl hooted a warning. A shadowy pair of bats swooped over his head.

Halloween is the one night of the year when black cats have strange powers. Spooky began to feel like a tiger. He bared his teeth and claws. He flattened his ears. He switched his tail. His hair stood on end.

Spooky went into the woods slinky-paw, slinky-paw, like a tiger stalking its prey. He made for the witch's hut under the witch hazel tree.

He scratched
at her door.
*Scritch,*
*scratch.*

When the door opened, Spooky saw that the white cat
was just behind the witch.
"*Pfft, Pfft!*" Spooky spat at the witch!

She answered with a laugh that sounded like an ogre crunching on bones.

She cackled. "So you want my new cat. She is only a ghost. She will become a real cat when I fly through the air without sitting on my broom. AND THAT WILL NEVER EVER HAPPEN! At midnight, I will round up my flock of bats and she shall ride behind me in your place, pussycat pet."

The witch slammed the door, keeping the white cat inside.

Spooky looked at her broom stand-
ing by the door. From his former life with
the witch, he knew how to work it.

He jumped on the handle. He dug his claws into it like a witch's sharp nails. He twisted his tail around it like a witch's crooked leg.

The broom began to move. *Swi-s-sh!* It flew around the witch hazel tree three times. *Thum-m-mp!* It bumped against the door.

The witch came out again.

Before she could open her mouth or shut the door, the broom swept her into the air. It swept her higher and higher. It swept her above the trees.

First Spooky was hanging by his front claws. Then he was hanging by his hind claws. And sometimes he was only hanging by his tail.

*Swoo-s-sh!* The broom gave the witch such a spank she went flying over the moon.

Spooky guided the broom back to the ground. The white cat was waiting for him. She was a real cat now because the witch had flown through the air without sitting on her broom. Spooky beckoned her to ride behind him.

He guided the broom to the Bascomb house. He and the white cat went one, two through the little door in the big door. They jumped up on the fat chair with the bump in the seat. They *pur-r-r, pur-r-r, pur-r-red* each other to sleep.

That is where the Bascomb mother found them in the morning. "Come quick, everybody!" she called.

They came quickly.

"It's like the white cat I saw," said the girl. "But this one is real. Somebody must have dropped her out of a car."

The boy went to a window, looked out and said, "There's only an old broom lying in the road."

"It looks like Spooky has a new friend," the girl said.
The mother agreed. "It looks like the Bascombs have a new pet."
Then Spooky opened his eyes and his whiskers twitched.